COMPOST, BY GOSH!

An Adventure with Vermicomposting

Written and Illustrated by
Michelle Eva Portman

Publisher's Cataloging-in-Publication
(Provided by Quality Books, Inc.)

Portman, Michelle Eva.
  Compost, by gosh! : an adventure with vermicomposting
/ written and illustrated by Michelle Eva Portman. --
1st ed.
    p. cm.
    SUMMARY : Rhyming text and vivid pictures augment this
introduction to the stages and benefits of worm
composting.
  ISBN 0-942256-16-6

  1. Earthworm culture--Juvenile literature.
2. Eisenia foetida--Juvenile literature. 3. Vermicomposting
--Juvenile literature. [1. Earthworms. 2. Compost.]
I. Title.
SF597.E3C66 2003   639'.75
                        QBI02-701976

Flower Press
10332 Shaver Road
Kalamazoo, Michigan 49024
ISBN 0-942256-16-6

For my beloved Etan, who encouraged me to enjoy my creativity; for my son Gaul, who encouraged me to teach children; and to my daughter Ella, for whom I wish, when given the chance to sit it out, will instead – dance!

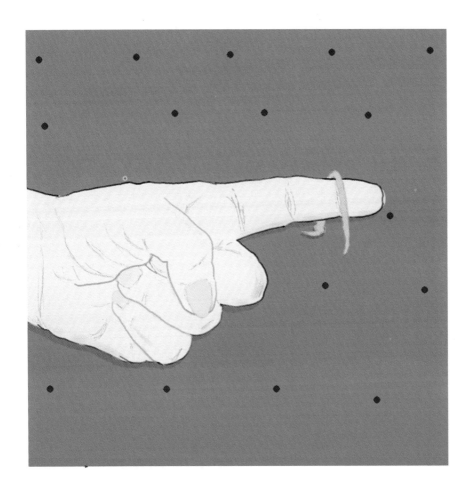

In a dark, plastic bin,
Where light rarely reaches,
Warm blackened earth
Was once berries and peaches.

As I open the lid,
I know what I'll find.
A drama unfolds
That boggles the mind.

Fuzzy mold grows,
As worms slither 'round.
Under wads of wet paper
Remnants of dinner are found.

Never quite stopping
The redworms continue,
Transforming all matter
From solid to sinew.

The peelings, the cores,
The stubs and the shells,
Now hard to make out
Among moisture and smells.

Hundreds and thousands
Of worms thrash about.
Through pits, stems and rinds,
They weave in and out.

While writhing and wriggling,
On food scraps they dined.
Now waste turned to gold
Has come out their behind.

They've made compost, by gosh,
That our plants and trees crave,
While enriching the soil,
Making fungi behave.

A plastic box was the start
That we needed no more.
We drilled holes on its sides,
Only not on its floor.

When we started the bin,
Of course nothing was there.
We added our food waste
And laid paper with care.

Then we sprayed water
'Til the paper was wet,
To make the best home
For a new kind of pet.

And the WORMS,
          yes we need them!
We placed some inside,
Then filled up the box
With leaves that had died.

Eisenia fetida (i see' nee a fet' id a),
Is our pet worms' real name.
They liked their new home.
They were quiet and tame.

The worms lived in darkness
For two months maybe three.

We fed them food garbage,
Even used bags of tea!

Soft peels and cores,
And soggy tomatoes,
Corn cobs and egg shells,
And skins of potatoes.

Apricots and nutshells,
And lettuce gone bad,
Spoiled grapes, squishy onions,
All the organics we had.

Then lo and behold,
We found a black muck.
That stuff that's called humus
Or compost, oh yuck!

We mixed the compost
Into every plant pot,
Then fuller and taller
And greener plants got.

As our plants grew
To be stronger and bigger,
We thanked our worm friends
For their hard work and vigor.

It was quite amazing,
The things they did do.
By digesting our waste,
They had made something new.

They turned waste to compost,
Food for plants and for trees,
That helps soil hold water,
Keeps grass from disease.

So we want you to know
By the end of this tale,
What you can do
With your bread crusts gone stale.

Your mushy brown pears
And soft wilted greens,
Carrot tops, pickle ends,
Your over-baked beans.

Your waste veggies and fruits
And unwanted dry toast—
Don't throw these away.
Make them into compost!

Composting Indoors with Worms (Vermicomposting)

Making compost using worms, called vermicomposting, is easy to do. You can vermicompost even if you live in an apartment or some other type of home with no yard. Composting is good for the environment. By recycling food waste, you can reduce waste disposal needs and costs. Use your compost instead of chemical fertilizers and pesticides.

To get started on your vermicomposting adventure you will need:

Adult help if you are a child.

A bin. Bins can vary in size and material type. However, the larger the bin, the more worms it will house and the more food waste they will eat. For indoor composting, a plastic box works well. The one in this book is a 73-quart (around a 70-liter) converted storage box. The bin will need to have small holes so that the worms and decomposing process will get lots of air. Worms love darkness, so the bin top should keep the light out.

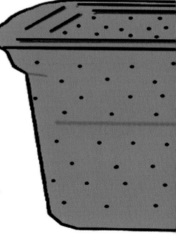

A place for your bin. The bin should be kept in a warm area that is always between 55° and 77° Fahrenheit (or between 13° and 25° Celsius). A closet, basement, utility room or garage would do fine.

Bedding. Shredded paper will work well as bedding for the worms. The paper holds moisture and also covers the food waste to minimize odors. The worms will eat the bedding (which should be at least 6 inches deep after moistening) along with the food waste. Newspaper, white office paper and dried leaves make excellent bedding material. Paper towels and napkins can also be used, but only if they don't contain synthetic materials, antibacterial agents or chemical cleaners.

Water is needed to moisten the bedding. Over time you may have to add moisture occasionally using a misting spray bottle. You will know it is too dry if the paper crinkles. If it gets too moist in the bin, you should add more dry bedding.

Worms. *Eisenia fetida,* also known as the redworm, is one species of worm commonly used for vermicomposting. (The worms found in the garden are usually not the type of worms that go in an indoor worm bin.) Redworms are usually sold by weight — about 600-1000 worms per pound (or per 0.45 kilogram). Worm suppliers will ship worms to you that will be happy living in your bin. You should not have to buy more worms once you get started. In fact, a properly balanced bin will produce enough worms to share with others. One pound of worms can consume one half to one pound (or 0.23 to 0.45 kilogram) of food waste a day and is a good amount of worms to start with if your bin is about the size of the one in this book.

Food. Left over fruits, vegetables, coffee grounds, and grains are the best food for the worms. Meat and dairy products are not recommended because they may cause bad odors. The food waste should be placed under the bedding material and not left on the surface. Be careful not to overfeed. You can give daily small feedings or less frequent larger feedings. Feed your worms lightly at first until the worms get accustomed to their new surroundings. If odors are a problem, there may be too much food and moisture in the bin. Stop feeding for a while and add more bedding.

To Harvest. Every 3 to 6 months take out the nutrient-rich worm castings that make up the compost. Mix the compost with soil and add it to your plants. Return the worms to the bin, add new bedding, more food, and let them compost, by gosh!

To learn more about vermicomposting you can read:

Wormology, Ross, M., Minneapolis, MN: Carolrhoda, Inc., 1996.

Worms Eat My Garbage: How to Set Up and Maintain a Worm Composting System, Appelhof, M., Second Edition, Kalamazoo, MI: Flower Press, 1997.

Worms Eat Our Garbage: Classroom Activities for a Better Environment, Appelhof, M., Fenton, M., Harris, B., Kalamazoo, MI: Flower Press, 1993.

Or watch the video:

Wormania!, Kalamazoo, MI: Flowerfield Enterprises with Billy B. Productions, 1995.

The End